Au

THE LIFT

RICHARD WEALE

Thank you for all your encouragement + support

Best wishes

Rachel x

THE LIFT

Published in United Kingdom 2021

by FGO Publications, Gloucestershire, England

Stories by their very nature are
creations of imagination and fantasy

ISBN 9798500842596

ONE
THE LIFT

Polly was late for work. Everything had been going wrong. She had slept through her alarm. How could that happen? She felt grimy, because in all the rush she hadn't had time to shower. Her stockings were laddered, snagged on something on the tube. And she had had to stand the whole way from Holborn.

Now she was waiting for the lift at her office building on Canary Wharf. It was a magnificent building that rose floor upon floor into the sky, as it dominated this part of the London horizon. She was involved in the most bizarre of conversations.

"Believe me lady, you don't want to catch this lift."

"Yes. I do."

"No Ma'am, you don’t" replied the smaller, thickset of the two, "not now, not this lift."

"But this is my lift. I work here."

"Not this lift Ma'am. Try later, or that one over there."

Polly wanted to scream, but she was still holding it together.

"Listen to me. This is my lift. I catch it every day. I am very late. I am catching this lift."

"Can't let you do that Ma'am."

"And stop calling me Ma'am. Are you Americans?" she asked in exasperation.

"No Ma'am, we are adventurers."

Polly paused for thought. They were two of the weirdest guys she had seen in a long time. It wasn't the brightly coloured purple, green, and orange hair and beards, or the alchemical symbols tattooed on their faces. It was their costumes. Like two guys from a SWAT team, but tie dyed instead of camouflage.

Perhaps that was their camouflage. Both men carried extra- large duffle bags.

"Gentlemen, I am catching this lift."

"Okay Ma'am," replied the smaller, who now accepted that the persistent woman was going to share their ride. He introduced himself as Walter. "And this is André," he said, indicating his considerably larger companion.

"Like the giant?"

"Yes, like the giant."

"Weird," she muttered, "who are these nutters?"

"Not nutters, Ma'am," said André, in a voice that was decidedly silken for a man of his stature, “adventurers."

"Adventurers with supersonic hearing?" she muttered again, blushing.

"Yes Ma'am, it comes in handy."

"On adventures?"

"Yes Ma'am."

Polly was saved from any more of this whack job conversation by the ding of the bell. The lift doors whispered open.

Standing either side of the door, the two mismatched, but identically dressed men bowed their heads and held out an arm, inviting her to enter first. With a few unexpected butterflies in her stomach, she stepped into the lift.

"I tell you what Ma'am," said Walter smoothly, "we'll even let you choose the button."

These guys are nutters, thought Polly, but said," It will be one hundred and four, that's my floor."

André turned to Walter and said in his silken voice, as if Polly wasn't there, "Why is this girl so rude?" To Polly he spoke nicely and slowly, as if explaining to a two-year old. “This morning, this lift, this trip, is different. We don't care which button you press. It's like your Alice."

"My Alice?" replied Polly now thoroughly confused.

"Yes, your Alice, Through the Looking Glass."

Polly realised he was referring to one of her favourite childhood books.

"How is it like my Alice?"

This time it was Walter who spoke. They were like a double act. "When she is in the corridor of a thousand doors it doesn't matter which one she goes through. It will be great. You are introducing an element of random spontaneity. I just normally close my eyes and press a button."

These guys are nutters, thought Polly. She imagined the shock on the trading floor when these two weirdos stepped out of the lift.

"You just don't get it," continued Walter, "and stop calling us nutters, we do have feelings you know."

Polly hung there in shock. Are they reading my thoughts?

`*Yes*,' came the silent reply, `*get used to it*.'

Polly didn't know whether to laugh or scream. This building had the fastest lift in London. She should have arrived at her floor ages ago. With all the weirdness, she hadn't noticed.

"We tried to warn you," the two men spoke together, musically, in harmony, like half of a barber shop quartet.

Simultaneously the two men reached down to their hold-alls, pulled the zips, and started removing and then attaching an assortment of weapons to themselves. Knives were strapped to calves, belts, and concealed in sleeves. Grenade like things were clipped to jackets and a collection of guns were held and strapped about their two persons.

"Ready?"

"Yep, ready."

"My God," squeaked Polly, now truly terrified, "are you terrorists?"

"No Ma'am," came the harmonious reply, "we already gone and told you, we are adventurers," and with that André handed her a strange looking pistol. "It's pretty simple, just point, pull the trigger and move on."

And with that, there was a loud ding, and the lift doors opened to reveal a flock of huge winged things tearing at a huge writhing Leviathan and with a shove in her back Polly stumbled into the nightmare.

"You did well Ma'am."

"If I did so goddamn well can I please graduate from Ma'am to Polly?"

"She did say please Walter," said André, "and she's more polite. Hasn't called us nutters for a while"

"Yes, okay," muttered Walter, "you are right, Polly it is."

They were sitting around a fire in a cave in a forest. The cave was warm and dry and André had told her it was safe. She trusted André. The day, if you could call it a day, had been the best day of her life.

They had come through into some kind of alien landscape. Polly knew it was alien because none of the creatures in front of her existed in the records of the Natural History Museum, or even in her worst nightmares. The twin suns in the sky whilst breath taking, reaching to her deepest heart with their beauty, were a suggestion that all was not well in the state of Elsinore.

A terrible keening wail had broken out from the flock. A dozen heads smeared with steaming guts pulled from the jerking body and held the trio with laser like fixation. The creatures resembled putrescent green vultures with long necks, the better to bury into their prey. But there the similarity ended. Instead of feathers they had lumpy skin that created unsettling patterns with the strange dual light sources, and instead of beaks they had small mouths full of sparkling razor sharp teeth. Almost as one they launched at the adventurers.

Polly didn't even think. She held her pistol in front of her and squeezed the trigger. An explosion of meat mid-air caught her conscious thought for a fraction of a second before she was shooting again. She was aware of Walter and André firing beside her and then the sky was full of exploding monsters.

In the unnatural calm that existed after, with ears humming from the concussions, a large hand patted her on the shoulder, making her jump.

"Way to go Ma'am."

She hoped they didn't notice the silent tear trickle down her cheek when Walter snapped the heels off her Jimmy Choo's, but as he so accurately observed, she wasn't exactly kitted out for this kind of adventuring.

"What do you mean, how does it work? It works."

"What? We don't get crushed by hyper-gravity, or breathe an atmosphere of sulphuric acid?"

"Not so far."

"Well that's ridiculous, impossible," said Polly, throwing a bone into the fire.

It was the best meal she had ever tasted, but she realised that owed more to her unlikely survival of multiple "adventures" today, than the quality of the meat or the chef's culinary skills. Not that Walter hadn't made a fine meal for them all.

"So, did you make the lift?"

"No Ma'am... sorry Polly," apologised Walter.

"But you're not human?"

"Define human?"

"Well generally being human doesn't come with the ability to converse psychically."

"Ah," hummed André, joining the conversation, "well, we are evolved."

"What from the future?"

André reached forward to tear a piece of meat from the spit, and turning to Walter, said, "You gotta admit Walter, this girl is pretty sharp."

Despite the compliment, Polly bristled at having slipped down the pole from Ma'am to girl, but decided to let it go.

"Well I sure am grateful for you two boys for saving my bacon today," she said, but looking at their good-natured faces, she could see that using irony on them was wasting her time. Not all of André's pouches held grenades, and reaching over she picked up another can of Coors and pulled the ring contentedly.

A light tap on her ankle brought Polly instantly alert.

`*Hostiles.*'

`*I thought you said it was safe*?' she mentally whispered into the pitch black.

`*Things change.*'

Her perspective on missing her shower "yesterday morning" had changed somewhat. Yesterday she had been attacked by monsters, trudged through stinking marshes, been covered in gore and blood, eaten some of the foul creatures that had been hunting them, and now slept in a cave full of smoke with two strange men. Her designer dress was stained and ripped and held in place by mud and stale sweat. All of this barely touched her consciousness as her hand felt the smooth stock of her new best friend and her finger caressed its trigger.

`*Okay, let's go.*'

Polly was surprised at how well she could see in the pitch-black cave. Her hearing too had become incredibly acute. Then she heard it. A slight slobber and wet rasp as something dragged itself on rock. The sound seemed to come from all around her. Lying on her back holding the pistol in both hands, she vainly stared up at the empty space above. That's when a huge dollop of slime landed on her face.

The gun in her hand exploded upwards with a volley of shots. There was a wet gasp, a moment of silence, and then all the breath went out of her as the massive corpse dropped from the roof of the cavern, and wetly and foully half crushed, half drowned her.

Polly opened her eyes. The bright light of the lift was broken by the concerned faces of Walter and André crouching over her.

"She's okay," they said simultaneously in their harmonious tones. And she was. Polly Granger really was okay.

Polly woke up with the sun streaming through the blinds of her apartment. She had had the most incredible dream. She felt dreadful though. Her head hurt, her sinuses were blocked, and she ached all over. Perhaps she had the flu. She would phone in and take the day off.

She eased her legs carefully out from under the silk duvet and planted them firmly on the bedroom floor. Yuk! What had she put her feet on? Looking down she saw the remains of the stinking, slimy, filthy dress she had bought in that little boutique in Chelsea. The "dream" all came back to her and with an involuntary yelp she curled up tight under the covers.

They met in a café on the King's Road. Polly ordered a cappuccino, an almond croissant, and wove her way over to where Walter and André were already sitting.

"How's the head?" Walter offered without preamble.

"Fine."

What was she doing here? she asked herself as she slid into the comfy couch.

`Because we invited you,'* came the reply, *`and you have discovered you have hidden talents.'

Polly blushed, but held Walter's gaze with a hard stare. "It's rude to invade my privacy like that."

Walter met her gaze for a few seconds before looking away.

"You're right, sorry. It's just that you are broadcasting like a beacon. We were trained as kids to differentiate between private and universal. I guess you don't have that."

"Can you teach me?"

"I guess so," replied Walter warily. "Is it worth the effort?"

"The effort?"

"Well it's only us."

"I'll teach you Polly," cut in André.

"Why thank you André," Polly said with a smile.

"Can we cut to the chase?" said Walter.

"And what exactly is the chase?"

"Polly you are good. With a bit of training you could be brilliant. We would like you to join us. We would like you to be an adventurer."

The first room André took her to was a high-end shooting range deep underground in the West End. Polly had been around enough to know that access to these kinds of executive facilities was not given to one and all. She said as much to Walter.

"We pulled in a favour or two. Our particular talents are well appreciated in certain influential circles."

Polly didn't care. She was having a great time. Night and day were a blur down here. She seemed to spend all her time mastering the art of pistol shooting, along with a variety of guns, some which would be recognised on the street, and some that may have escaped out of the wildest dreams of fevered minds.

The snooker hall, or to be totally accurate, former snooker hall, was next. Here, she spent time with André, mastering the art of combat with and without weapons. She learnt that anything could be utilised as a weapon. A paper cup, a girl's hair ribbon, and Polly's favourite, a fountain pen. As she had tartly said to André, she could write with it as well.

Her preferred choice was a short doubled edged blade, but she loved them all. André had told her she had a real gift for the crossbow, but it was the guns she loved. Walter and André both said ladies–they knew better than to say girls–were the best shots. Something to do with lack of ego. They didn't have anything to prove, just exercised their talent. Polly, apparently, was a natural. Her grouping was consistently brilliant and whether with a pistol or assault rifle she was formidably accurate, fast and smooth. And even without any training, they'd witnessed how she could function under pressure.

There were certain benefits too. Polly hadn't worked since her first adventure. Walter and André had insisted she take a serious bank transfer so she could concentrate on her training. Adventures weren't all monster infested wastelands. Sometimes adventures were sources of abundance.

She had loved her job as a senior Accounting Executive in Docklands and had been quite sad when she told her boss she was leaving for personal reasons. He had even offered her a raise to stay. It was nice to be appreciated.

One evening, Walter, Polly and André were having dinner at a charming little Italian restaurant in Islington. Very unpretentious, with excellent food and good service. Fun and friendly, it was one of her favourites.

Just as her bruschetta arrived, who should walk in the door, but Phillip, her ex-boyfriend from two years ago, with a bunch of his mates. Phillip hadn't been a gentleman, in fact he had treated her badly and she wasn't pleased to see him.

He saw her straight away and sauntered over in that cocky self-assured way she remembered so well.

"Hello, Polly." The syllables were drawn out and over loud. For the first time he seemed to notice Walter and André, but still seemed confident and brash. "Who are your friends? Your new Fan Club?"

Polly looked him straight in the eyes. Her smile was lovely but her eyes hard and cold. "Phillip, I don't want to talk to you, please go away."

Phillip was confused. He had always dominated Polly. He liked to humiliate her in front of his friends and slap her around in private. However, even a bully as arrogant and insensitive as Phillip could sense all was not as it should be. Still, his mates were watching. He reached forward and put his hand roughly on her shoulder and hissed, "Be nice bitch."

Both Walter and André had stood up, but André's tuition of Polly had been very thorough. With a fluid motion, she rose as if to embrace Phillip, placed her hands on the sides of his head, and drove her thumb nails into the lobes of his ears, crushing them against the sides of his skull. Phillip screamed like a child as he dropped to his knees in pain. Like all bullies he could dish it out but struggled to take it.

The restaurant was silent now except for Phillip's squeals and profanities.

As Phillip paused his screaming to draw breath, a silken voice by her side spoke, filling the expectant restaurant with its rich timbre, "You heard the lady. She doesn't want to talk to you."

Polly released her grip and Phillip knelt in front of her like a supplicant, holding his agonised ears. Walter, who had been watching Phillip's friends, indicated to them with a nod that they should take their buddy and leave.

Polly straightened her dress and sat down, smiling as a ripple of applause pealed out from the other diners.

"Friend of yours?" asked André, raising his glass in a mock salute.

"Never seen him before in my life," replied Polly with a smile.

Polly was waiting for the lift with Walter and André. If anything, her addition made them look even odder. André was something of a giant, and Walter was small and stocky but both of them were hard looking men. Polly was slight, and rather out of place. They were all dressed identically in the tie-dyed SWAT gear, which identified them as a team, and added to the bizarreness of it all. Three large holdalls rested tidily by the lift doors.

“Polly? It is you?" It was Felicity, a junior accountant from her old department, who stared unbelieving at Polly.

"Hello Felicity, you’re in early."

It had been Polly's idea to arrive hours before the usual time work started, to avoid this very kind of thing. There were slots of time when the lift became a transporter. Polly couldn't imagine what happened to any poor sod who took the lift during these seemingly random moments.

"Yes,” said Felicity. “Mr Theatcher gave me a load of invoices to process, and they have to be done by lunch time."

"But Felicity, it's four a.m!"

"I know, I know, but you know what he's like."

Unfortunately, Polly did know what he was like and sympathised.

"What happened to you Polly? You just disappeared with some rumour of personal problems."

For the first time she looked Polly up and down and then studied her two companions. "And what in God's name are you wearing? You look like you left Vietnam and morphed into hippies."

Polly's appearance had always been feminine. Normally she was seen in the latest Paris fashions, with her hair cut by Spyros or Luigi at their Mayfair salon. Now she looked tough and fit, and although her hair was clean and sparkled, it was tied back in a simple pony tail.

All this time Walter and André had stood silent and still, like disembodied mutes.

"Aren't you going to introduce me to your friends?"

However, at that moment Polly was rescued by the polite ding of the arriving lift, whose doors silently opened. She leant forward giving Felicity a slight peck on the cheek.

"Lovely to see you darling, we must meet for lunch," and with that she picked up her heavy holdall and the three of them were gone.

Walter had asked her for a random number between one and fifty and she had picked her age. When the lift doors opened into a smart lobby, for the first second Polly thought the lift hadn't worked.

On the back wall was a reception desk. Polly gulped when she saw the thing "manning" the desk. It was tall, well dressed and had a purplish face covered with little waving tubes that whistled melodically. Polly wasn't aware of speaking 'whistle,' but she clearly understood its question, "Can I help you please?"

Polly started to panic and turned back to re-enter the lift, but was stopped short, by a purple hand on her arm, and her reflection in the mirror on the lift wall. It was the same tie-dyed camo-gear, but her face looked like it would be happier on a coral reef and Polly's heart skipped a beat.

`*Keep it together Polly,*' came a whisper in her mind. `*This is a moment for calm, rational thought, and diplomacy.*'

Polly was fighting the urge to scream, but remembering André's lessons, she took a deep breath in, a long exhale, and turning around, stepped with her two companions back into the lobby.

TWO
FIVE YEARS LATER

Polly watched the Rocky Mountains passing below her. Wow, they were so beautiful. They seemed to go on and on for ever. She sipped her champagne, and again, for the thousandth time, thanked the universe for putting her together with Walter and André so long ago.

That chance meeting, or was it chance, had changed her existence forever. Three or four times a year the three of them went on adventures. An incredible, indescribable series of experiences that had changed her in such a good way. Always a confident woman, now she felt she could deal with anything.

She was also, by Earth standards, an incredibly wealthy woman, although luckily, she felt that her fortune hadn't changed her. It was the adventures that had done that.

In her old world she had lived well, wore fine clothes, travelled when she could. Now she always flew first class. She was on her way to San Francisco where she had a lovely home in the Haight. How she loved the Haight.

She had beautiful homes in a dozen spectacular places around the world. Gothenburg, Siena, and Queenstown were particular favourites, and of course she still had a home in London.

She sighed and switched on her television. She didn't have time in her life to waste on TV, but she liked to catch up with the latest movies. She put on the lovely leather padded noise cancelling headphones, and settled back with a romantic comedy.

"We interrupt this movie, with startling news from London."

She watched in amazement as pictures of Canary Wharf in London came up. Behind a harried reporter from the BBC, there seemed to be a battle going on. Cars were exploding, buildings collapsing, and armed police in Kevlar vests and helmets were firing bursts of automatic fire at something.

Oh my God, Polly thought, blood draining from her face. The camera clearly showed the source of the mayhem. It was humanoid, in so far as it had two arms, two legs and a head, but that was where the resemblance to humanity ended. Its armour covered chest was bigger and broader than a grizzly bear's, and it stood twenty feet tall in its shining though scuffed metallic boots . The gaping slit of its mouth, lined with savage scything teeth, roared out its challenge as the cannon in its giant arms caused cars, trucks, and nearby buildings, to explode. But it was the single clear word that the monster was screaming, that had made her blood run cold...

"POLLY!"

William Farringway was the Prime Minister's liaison with the Intelligence services and Special Forces. He was having a very trying day, but he spoke calmly into the telephone.

"No, Prime Minister. No, we don't know what it is. My best guess, ruling out a demon from hell, would be some type of alien."

“Well no, Prime Minister, generally demons don't come armed with some kind of laser cannon.”

“Yes, Prime Minister, we have scrambled the SAS, the SBS, Anti-Terrorist squad, everyone basically, Prime Minister.”

“No, Prime Minister, I have no idea why it is yelling Polly.”

“Thank you, Prime Minister, I'll keep you informed."

Walter and André were in Hanoi having breakfast. Waffles. André loved waffles, and wherever they went on Earth, he loved to have them for breakfast. They loved the Earth. It was jam packed full of beauty, great food, and culture. Hanoi was not an easy place to get waffles, but then André was a very particular man.

The television over the counter suddenly switched to a breaking story. Walter, who had been half following it, spoke in rapid Vietnamese to the owner to turn up the volume.

"Oh shit," said André, around a mouthful of waffle, "that's not good."

Alfred Smith was a sergeant in the Special Air Service. That meant he was one of the guys who made things happen. The Ruperts, as the Officers were known, unlike in other branches of the military, took a step back from operational effectiveness.

With a name like Alfred, in a place where piss taking was a way of life, Alfred took a lot of stick. Fortunately, he quite liked his nickname. In a job where you killed people for a living, dealing with a bit of stick was like salve on an open wound.

So, when the scramble call came, “Tupper” Smith was

in the Red Lion in Hereford having a pint with Gonzo. Krishna "Gonzo" Bhatri had come from the Gurkhas and had passed selection first time. He had met with Tupper during training in Borneo, and by some lucky fate, the two friends had managed to be posted together.

Now years later, Tupper was leader of their squad. The two had served all over, fighting the government's secret wars, and now spent most of their time undercover, fighting Jihad.

By the time they got back to the base, the first response unit had already left for London. Tupper, Gonzo and the rest of the squad were being briefed by one of the Ruperts. No one wore insignia of rank, but the plummy voice of an expensive education was more associated with the officer class. Not a golden rule, Tupper knew. Many good men chose to serve as non-commissioned officers in the Regiment because they wanted to fight at the sharp end.

Tupper thought he was beyond surprise, but the news coverage of the thing at Canary Wharf gave him a squeeze of tension right down in his gut. Bloody hell, it was like something out of a movie.

Still calm and unflappable on the outside, he asked, "What intel do we have?"

"Basically none. This is it. CCTV showed it coming out of a lift of the big tower, the one with one hundred and ten floors. It came out yelling and shooting."

"And what, or who, is Polly?"

Polly was stuck on an aircraft travelling to San Francisco. She was trying to maintain calm. Those early lessons with André helped. She controlled her breathing, emptied her mind, and felt her heart rate return to normal. After all, she wasn't actually under threat. Well she was, but not now, at this moment.

When she'd seen Sam on the television screen, she knew she was in deep trouble. That was what they'd called him, because even with the metamorphosis that sometimes took place, none of them could pronounce his name.

Sam was dead. That's what kept running through her mind. But clearly Sam was not dead, he was there in London, and severely pissed off.

"Yes, Prime Minister. I know, Prime Minister. Yes, it's untenable Prime Minister. The SAS will be onsite in fifteen minutes Prime Minister. Yes, the Americans have offered assistance Prime Minister. I'll keep you informed Prime Minister."

William Farringway put down the phone, swearing under his breath. Holy shit. What just hit London? "The Thing." A Sci Fi buff, he was already thinking of it, as "The Thing From Outer Space," was marching across London blowing up everything in its path. At least one bus full of passengers had exploded, and the death toll was accelerating. The Thing seemed impervious to bullets.

Farringway picked up the direct line to Hereford. "Hello Charles, yes it's a disaster zone here, are you getting it on satellite? Have your boys got any anti-tank missiles in those choppers? Then get the second unit to stop at Brize Norton to pick some up, this bastard is indestructible."

Polly had left the airport as if nothing had happened. Travelling first class had its advantages. She settled back in the deep comfort of the limousine's leather seats, as it wound its way through the San Franciscan streets, and tried to ease the tension in her stomach. She ignored the chilled bottle of wine in the ice bucket, and the crystal decanters of single malt, and sipped water from a beautiful Venetian glass.

Her phone on the seat beside her vibrated, and she smiled at the identifying picture.

"Hi, Walter, how's it going?" she purred in a steady voice.

"Polly, have you seen the news?" Walter replied, in his off-world drawl.

"Sam?"

"Yes," he said, relieved he hadn't had to break the news.

"He seems pretty pissed off. Seems to be demolishing half of London."

"He seems to be travelling in a straight line, any idea where he's going?"

"At a guess, my flat."

"Where are you now Polly?"

"In the car, on the way home."

"Which one Polly?"

"Haight Ashbury."

"Well he won't get there in a hurry."

"Don't underestimate him Walter."

"Well he can hardly just jump on a flight at Heathrow."

"Don't worry Walter. This is Sam we are talking about. He'll find a way."

"Look after yourself Polly."

"Sure Walter. Love to André," and with that she cut the

call, sank back into the seat and enjoyed the views of the San Franciscan streets.

Sergeant Alf “Tupper” Smith sat with his team in the Sea King helicopter, studying the data stream on the Thing, which was currently making its way across London. With the hatch open it was cold, and the sound of the rotors would be deafening without the headsets they all wore.

It seemed to be heading in a straight line northwest through the East End. It was devastating Stepney at the moment.

"It sure likes blowing shit up."

"Where do you think it's heading?"

"Who knows? Shoreditch, Islington, Birmingham? How much stamina has it got?"

"We RV at Victoria Park. The 4x4's are already waiting."

"Can't we have Humvees?" asked Gonzo.

"I wish," replied Tupper as he saw an explosion in an upper story of a tower block. What the hell are we going into, he thought.

"Yes, Prime Minister."

"We have been offered support by Washington, Prime Minister."

"Yes, I know it looks bad Prime Minister."

"Thank you, Prime Minister."

Farringway put the phone down, his patience beginning to wear a little thin. Like all professionals at a high level, he saw politicians come and go. Mostly capable people. If you got to the position where you were running a country and dealing with the complexities of International intrigue, war, and terrorism, you needed to be fit for the job. Not that that was universally true. To be fair, the current Prime Minister maintained a calm head and could make credible decisions in a crisis. But having some monster marching across London shooting and blowing up everything in its path certainly made a change from the budget and the Syrian crisis.

He pressed a button on the intercom on his desk. "Have the lads from Hereford arrived yet?"

"ETA three minutes, Sir."

Polly entered the key code, disabling the security system, and made herself a pot of tea. She remembered the conversation with Walter about her up-to-the-minute security system.

"You install a retinal scanner, the next thing you know, some bastard will cut your eye out with a grapefruit spoon."

"But surely it wouldn't work, the scanner would detect the trauma."

"Yeah, precisely. Bit late for your eye though."

He had a point, and Polly had gone for a keypad.

Her phone beeped, and it was André.

"Any news?"

"Only what's on the TV."

“We have heard from certain friends, that Special Forces have been called out."

"Well, good luck for them then," said Polly, pityingly.

"What about collateral damage?"

Tupper was in a three-way conversation with Farringway and the Colonel at Hereford.

"Just stop the thing," said Farringway. "It's causing mass destruction. It's done more damage in the last hour than all other threats since the Blitz."

"Where are you now?"

"We are going to intercept it near Weavers Fields."

Tupper watched calmly as an abandoned shopping trolley bounced off the bumper as the Range Rover accelerated down the deserted pavement. The roads were full of silent cars left by panicked owners who had sought sanctuary underground in the city's metro system.

They could hear the concussions of explosions getting closer now, and for the last time Tupper went through his inner checklist, then gave his final instructions to the team.

Walter and André had called in a favour. The jet that was accelerating down the runway leaving Hanoi had only two passengers. The flight attendant, dressed not in a stylish uniform, but in expensive distressed jeans and a Dolce and Gabbana silk top, handed Walter a glass of bourbon and André, tomato juice.

"Might as well make the most of it," said Walter.

"When do we arrive in Los Angeles?" asked André in his quiet voice.

"Sixteen hours normally, but it may be less."

"Then we'll start with dinner please."

"Yes Sir," replied the Stewardess, "I'll bring you the menu."

"STOP!"

It had been Tupper's idea, so he had been given the job. Dropped off in the Thing's path with a portable PA system, and nothing else.

He had waited on the roof of a prominent block of flats, watching the wave of destruction approach. He had set up the speakers facing towards the Thing. They were military issue and seriously loud. British made, they had been used by the Yanks at Waco to broadcast psychologically destructive noise at the soon to be removed residents. Tupper had been there as an advisor. Today he had a different strategy.

The neighbouring tower block was rocked by an explosion, and Tupper kept down as debris ricocheted around him. Jumping up in clear sight, he stood on the roof edge of the twenty-story building. He could see the Thing below, about a quarter of a mile away, raise its laser cannon, and shouted into the microphone, "STOP. LET'S TALK ABOUT POLLY."

And unbelievably, the Thing stopped.

"Yes, Prime Minister."

"It was our man's idea."

"I know we don't negotiate with terrorists Prime Minister."

"It's already working, Prime Minister. It's all down to our man. Apparently, we *do* negotiate with aliens."

Polly was glued to her TV.

The whole world was glued to the TV as the news feed came in from London. Initially the news organisations had tried helicopters, but the thing had shot them down. Then a BBC crew of a camera man and female anchor had got onto the roof of Polly's old work building on Canary Wharf, where the monster had emerged. They had been filming the initial mayhem. Now with the best telephoto lens money could buy, the BBC was broadcasting crystal clear images of exploding buildings, lorries, and buses. Burning buildings, sirens wailing. It was great. If only the monster was more visible. That's where social media kicked in. In any conflict, there is always some tough kid or two, willing to risk their lives to put out video of what's really going on.

When the TV stations are beholden to the politicians, this footage rarely sees the light of day. Today it was skilfully mixed into the news feed by the talented editors at Broadcasting House.

For a long time now, TV news had been about suffering served up as entertainment, and today this truly *was* entertainment.

Polly watched aghast as a man dressed in black fatigues, tough, weathered, and Polly thought, good looking, stood on the edge of a roof, and yelled out her name. The shot switched to Sam, who had stopped walking, stopped firing, looked up at the tiny figure on the roof, and bellowed, "OKAY."

Then the screen went blank.

"Polly, you're screwed."

It was Walter on the phone. This was her special phone. This phone wasn't really a phone, it just looked like one. Good enough to satisfy airport security, if needs be it could make network calls, but Walter and André were far too suspicious and careful to actually use normal forms of communication.

It had long been on the public record, that all calls on the planet were monitored. Everybody's whereabouts at all times was known, to less than a metre from their phone’s location software. The TV in the front room had a microphone that broadcast whatever it heard.

Even domestic appliances had such technology installed. “Good,” and “bad” people can switch on the camera and microphone on your smart phone. Everyone knew it, and no one cared. Living in the twenty first century requires practiced stupidity.

Walter and André cared, which is why Polly's phone was truly secure.

"They're negotiating with Sam. He certainly has got their attention. He must be seriously pissed off with you."

"Can you pull in any favours?"

"Are you kidding? The Brits or the Yanks will give you up. Polly, Sam just destroyed half of London."

"What shall I do?"

"Get out, Polly. Just to be sure, shower, wear new clothes, only carry cash, use the stealth veil, steal a car. We land in six hours. Meet at the cabin."

Polly put the phone down. She wasn't panicked, just calm and matter of fact. She moved with precise urgency. Stripping off, she tidily hung her Moschino dress in the closet, knowing she would never see it again.

Stepping out of the shower, she towelled herself dry, then took the sealed plastic packages from the back of the wardrobe. She remembered Walter years ago insisting that in each of her homes she should have this sorted. She loved these guys, and rightly trusted everything they had taught her.

Breaking the seal, she took out the plain, nondescript but functional camos, and got dressed. As she laced up her new boots, she looked around her beautiful home for the last time, put on her new hat with the fine mesh veil that would hopefully confuse the thousands of cameras, pulled on her latex like gloves, and without a look back silently closed the door behind her.

Walter and André had landed at Los Angeles LAX. Landing in a private jet does have some advantages when you want to pass unnoticed, but today, security was going through the roof.

The customs agent stared up at André, comfortably dressed in a soft Armani suit. When not on adventures their hair and beards were naturally coloured, but the strange symbols tattooed on André's and Walter's faces were quite disturbing. André held his gaze with bored indifference.

"Reason for visit?"

"Pleasure," replied André in his gentle voice. "Catching a 49ers game, then down to Vegas to see Bette singing, and play the tables."

The customs officer was used to dealing with high

rollers, but there was something a little off about these two guys. Still, everything seemed to be in order.

Nothing had flashed about their passports. It would have been surprising if they had, but still, an alert had been sent to a smart phone in Washington, and a very worried man, watching a monitor showing events in the UK, had made a link to these two new arrivals in the USA.

"Yes, Prime Minister."

"We have run checks. There was a Polly Granger who has a home in Islington, which was directly on the pathway."

"Yes, Prime Minister. Her last place of work was at Stockdon Trading on the 104th floor of the Peter Tower at Canary Wharf."

"Yes, Prime Minister, the one the alien came out of."

"Now, Prime Minister? I understand she is currently in San Francisco. She arrived there by plane a few hours ago."

"From Sweden, Prime Minister. She has homes in both places, and others around the world."

"Yes, it is a mystery, Prime Minister. There is no family money. She suddenly resigned from her job five years ago. She seems to have come into a lot of money recently, looking at the properties she now owns around the globe."

"Dodgy, Prime Minister. There seems to be no evidence of that. However, there is one thing."

"Apparently, after she left her job, she had a pass to use the firing range under Whitehall."

"Yes, I know Prime Minister. Yes, it does seem like a security nightmare. Apparently, she has some very influential friends."

"I wouldn't want to compromise you with the details Prime Minister."

"Yes, I understand that Prime Minister, I know you are responsible for running the country. I will be at Downing Street in thirty minutes, to brief you in person."

"Thank you, Prime Minister."

The advantage of 21st century top end cars with their sophisticated electronics, enhanced with gadgets supplied by Walter and André, meant stealing cars was incredibly easy. One press of a button and the security and ignition systems were reprogrammed.

The skill was doing it unobserved, quickly switching

number plates, and not picking something so rare it would stand out. Something like a Mercedes or a Lexus would be okay. Polly knew where there was a nice Porsche SUV, which would be handy in the Park. They were pretty common in California, although Polly, being a purist, was appalled at the very notion of them.

Still it would function very nicely, and it was a five-hour drive to Yosemite, so she might as well be comfortable. Her device contained all her favourite music, and Polly switched on the sound system and settled in for a beautiful drive.

She opened the cabin door to the smells and sizzle of bacon cooking, and wood smoke from the range.

Walter, dressed impeccably in a beautiful suit, wearing a Tweetie Pie apron to protect it from splashes, grabbed Polly in a big hug.

"How're you doing, Ma'am?"

Polly fixed him with a steely eye.

"Just kidding, Polly. Any issues?"

"No. How did you get here so fast? Where's André?"

"Good. Usual shenanigans. Out back, chopping wood."

Polly knew Walter would only give her information he considered relevant to their mission.

"So, what's the mission?"

It was Walter's turn to give Polly a long hard look. "Survival."

Sergeant Alf "Tupper" Smith looked across the floor of the gigantic transport plane at the Thing sitting on the bench. The giant monster was the most terrifying thing he had ever seen. It had a huge gash mouth full of scything teeth. Tupper couldn't work out how it could speak so clearly, and how in God's name it was speaking English. It was a long flight to the West Coast. No need to land at LAX, they were destined for a secret military base somewhere in California.

Gonzo and the rest of his unit were sat on his side of the plane. Tupper missed the normal banter. If their guest had been a SEAL or from Delta Force there would have been a deal of piss taking going on. He wasn't surprised that no one was baiting the Thing.

"Do you have a name?" asked Tupper in the end.

The sound that came out was like static, which lasted about ten seconds. The great maw broke into the scariest grin Tupper could imagine, and the monster spoke in its clear English voice.

"Precisely. That's why Polly called me Sam."

The eyes looking at Tupper had orange irises and a slit pupil that had echoes of its slash maw. The closest eyes on Earth that Tupper could relate to were of a crocodile, or alligator. He had wrestled a croc once for a bet. It had not been one of his better ideas, and in the end had only been resolved with his blade. He winced in remembrance. That croc was like Bambi compared to Sam.

Tupper though had noticed a change in its eyes, they were excited.

"What's up?" he asked.

"We are getting close."

"How do you know?"

"I can smell her!"

Polly and André were playing chess. They were sat comfortably in front of the fire, sipping their tonic waters. That was the only clue really, that they weren't just vacationers.

`*We could be religious nuts, or just health nuts,*' said Walter in her mind.

"Please Walter, will you stop doing that."

Polly had never fully got used to Walter and André's telepathic abilities.

"I thought André had taught you how to shield. How to distinguish between private and broadcast."

"I was concentrating on the game."

"Polly, Polly, we have taught you better than that. Wake up girl."

Polly was just about to reply when there was a loud rap at the door. Polly walked the short distance to the door and opened it.

`*POLLY*!' André and Walter yelled in her mind together, but it was too late. Blocking out the light, a huge scythe toothed grin on his face, stood Sam, holding a bunch of flowers. The incongruity of it didn't register. Polly slammed the door of the cabin, yelling out, "Shit, it's him." But there was no need, Walter and André already knew.

At that moment there were twin explosions, so close together an amateur would think it was one, and Tupper and Gonzo, burst through the back door.

"ENOUGH." With a huge clap of his hands André bellowed like an old God of Valhalla, and time froze. Then there was a blinding flash of light, and everything changed.

"What the bloody hell just happened?"

"You have died, then come to heaven. Please prepare for the afterlife."

"You're kidding me, right?"

Polly, who was the beneficiary of many adventures, had a very fast snap on reality, and its infinite number of sensory permutations.

She was pretty impressed with the guy, who she recognised from her TV, to orientate himself so fast, considering they were sat on a bench in one of the busiest space ports in Andromeda.

"Yeah, I'm just messing with you," said Polly. "You had better hide that under the bench," Polly nodded at the machine pistol Tupper was gripping with white knuckle intensity. "This is essentially like an airport terminal, and we don't want security thinking you're a terrorist."

She held out a firm, yet well-manicured hand. "Hi, I'm Polly."

"I'm perfectly aware who you are Miss Granger."

The sight of a family of Frebans gliding along beside their luggage, was the straw that broke the camel's back.

"For God's sake Polly," he said in a softened tone, "what the fuck is going on?"

"So, you have me at a disadvantage," said Polly. "You seem to know all about me, and you haven't introduced yourself. I'm guessing Special Forces, and you seem to be working with Sam, despite him blowing up half of London."

"Well, because he blew up half of London." Instantly transported half way across the universe, Tupper could see little value in maintaining security. It was obvious he was going to have to trust this girl if he was ever going to have a pint in the Red Lion again. "We couldn't touch him, bullets, grenades, anti-aircraft missiles, nothing. So, I tried diplomacy, and amazingly it worked."

"You mean, you gave me up, a British subject, to a marauding alien."

"Yeah, that's about it."

They were sat in a café sharing a pot of unidentifiable beverage, which didn't taste too bad under the circumstances. Tupper hadn't convinced himself to try the food yet, which mostly seemed alive, slimy, and wriggling.

"So, who came up with that scenario?"

"What scenario?"

"Sam standing at the front door with a bunch of flowers, whilst you bastards blew the back-door in."

“Sam.”

"He didn't!"

"He did."

Polly's beautiful face went a deeper shade of red, and for the first time in twenty-four hours Tupper burst out laughing.

He held out his hand. "Alf “Tupper” Smith, Sergeant in the SAS, Earth Alien Liaison Officer, and matchmaker."

"Yes, Prime Minster"

"Yes. Disappeared, Prime Minister."

"Yes, we had them under surveillance. Satellite, perfect optics, and thermal imaging."

"Yes, the girl, Prime Minister, her two companions, yes the ones I told you about, very helpful chaps, and two of our boys from Hereford."

"Just vanished, Prime Minister."

"I don't know if Scotty did beam them up, Prime Minister. It's as good a guess as I have, Prime Minister.”

"The alien, Prime Minister? No, I am afraid it was left behind. No, it's not very happy, Prime Minister."

"No, Prime Minister, neither are the Americans."

"How did you find me?"

"Smell."

"Smell?"

"Smell!"

"You're kidding."

"No."

"From how far away?"

"Well not from England. In London he was going in a straight line to your apartment. I don't know, we didn't talk about it. Coming over in a Hercules transport, at 37,000 feet, Sam picked you up when we were flying over the Rocky Mountains."

"Wowza," muttered Polly.

"Yeah, that was pretty much my reaction."

Polly and Tupper had moved from the spaceport café, to a bar on the edge of the terminal, and were having a drink.

"So, you seem to know your way around. Have you been here before?"

"No," said Polly, gazing coolly into his eyes. They were interesting eyes. She detected laughter and warmth in those eyes, but also the cold seriousness of a warrior. A warrior who has lived a life of war, taking many lives. They were complicated, but she detected a beauty and honesty in them. She liked those eyes, which smiled so readily, and seemed to radiate a kind of magic.

"But you weren't surprised. You have been to places like this before?"

"Yes," she replied, "many times."

"How the hell is that possible?"

"It's a long story."

"I think we have the time."

"I'm not sure I know you well enough. I'm not sure I trust you. You after all are the Earth Alien, what did you call yourself?"

"Liaison Officer."

"Precisely, you work for the bad guys."

"I work for Her Majesty's Government."

"Exactly, how bad can it get?"

"So, what did you do, jilt him at the altar?"

"Who?"

"Sam, of course."

"I don't know what the hell is going on with Sam."

"He went to an awful lot of trouble to bring you flowers."

"Lay off, will you. There is no history between Sam and I."

"You could have fooled me."

"Well, of course, we have history, just not the romantic kind. You have seen him. I can honestly say, and expect it to be universally accepted, he's not my type."

"And what is your type," asked Tupper, holding her attention with those dancing eyes.

Polly returning his gaze calmly, hoping he couldn't detect the glisten on her skin, and the quickening in her heart.

Gonzo was also in a bar at the spaceport on Andromeda.

Like his comrade in arms, Gonzo was a hard man. A Gurkha. The Nepalese people had been serving the British army for generations. Growing up in Nepal, on the rooftop of the Earth, had been tough. It was a poor country. As a child he had marvelled at the rich fat westerners who came to his homeland to find themselves, and to climb its mountains.

When he had gone to England for selection, the West had seemed like a land of aliens, and he remembered the feeling of unease when, alone and excited, he had explored the seedy side of London night life.

But that hadn't prepared him for this. He was sat in a shady alcove, drinking with the two weirdos. They were okay. It was all the other freaks and bug-eyed monsters that were causing Gonzo trouble.

He had taken to Walter and André straight away. He didn't trust them. He didn't know them. After a life in the Regiment there were men he trusted implicitly with his life, but there was something about the two friends, parallels of experience, like fellow travellers met on a journey, that resonated with him.

"So, what's the story?" asked Walter, "how come you're working with Sam."

"Hey, I'm just a grunt," replied Gonzo. "I just do as I'm told."

"Come on man," said André in his gentle, confident voice, "don't give us the hard act. Does it look like we're drowning you, or pulling your finger nails out?"

"No," admitted Gonzo. "Are you going to?" he asked with a smile.

"Come on man," repeated André, "we're all friends here."

"How is Charles?" enquired Walter from left field.

"Charles, who the hell is Charles?" asked Gonzo, wondering if this was some kind of interrogation technique.

"Oh, come on man," said André for the third time, "you know. Charles. He's the Man. We go way back, us and Charles."

Brad Kitzanger was a Navy SEAL. He was having an interesting day. Kitzanger didn't have good or bad days. Every day was an interesting day, but it wasn't everyday he was babysitting a giant alien, who looked like he had stepped out of a John Carpenter movie, had recently destroyed half of London, and was seriously pissed off.

"I need to get back to London."

The alien spoke in a calm but urgent way, in that goddamn irritating Limey accent. How was that possible, wondered Kitzanger, for the umpteenth time. It was disconcerting enough that he spoke such perfect English in the first place. Kitzanger had been on assignment at the London Embassy on multiple occasions, and the Brits' goddamn superior lah-di-dah ways got right under his skin.

"Why?" asked Kitzanger.

"Polly has gone, and her friends, and the soldiers."

"What do you mean gone?"

"Gone, left, vanished."

"From the US?" said Kitzanger incredulously.

"From the planet," replied the alien, as if to a child. "Gone."

"Yes, Prime Minister."

"Yes, Prime Minister. According to the alien, the girl, her friends, and our men have left the Earth."

"The alien, Prime Minister. He wants to come back to London."

"Yes, I know Prime Minister, it could be a nightmare situation. I wouldn't know about a PR nightmare, Prime Minister."

"As I understand it Prime Minister, he wants to leave."

"Not London, Prime Minister, Earth."

"Yes, that would be a good thing, Prime Minister."

"Thank you, Prime Minister. I'll keep you informed."

In Washington D.C. George Bewley had been busy making phone calls.

Finally, a patient female voice said, "The President will speak to you now."

George was pleasantly surprised at the suddenness of his connection. He was a professional who had held his place at the Agency for a long time. Retired from the field, he now oversaw Global Covert Operations for his great country's fight for survival in a hostile world.

Over the decades, both in the field and behind a desk he had had some interesting allies, but none more so than the two who had recently landed in a private jet at LAX. It couldn't be a coincidence.

Walter and André's physical and sartorial appearance hadn't changed one jot since George first came upon them in a Seoul bar in 1952. Always weird, always dapper, they seemed to blend in despite André's huge frame. Their gift with languages helped. Wherever in the world George had run into them, Walter and André always spoke the local language with an easy fluency, as if they had been born there.

It was in Vietnam in the late sixties that Walter had first approached him with his offer of assistance in certain areas, in return for a few favours. Now sixty years later, George was in his nineties, wiry and eagle eyed, despite his advanced years. He was way past official retirement, but still a powerful force in the machinations of hidden influence. He wistfully noted that Walter and Andre looked the same now as the first time he'd seen them.

"Yes, Mr. President. I wonder if I could come over for a meeting. Something has come up."

"Yes Mr. President, it is related to the Alien."

In the twenty-three years that George had been Director of the Agency, he still got a buzz of awe and excitement in the Oval Office. He had served four Presidents, and, he suspected this would be his last.

"You wanted to discuss something with me George."

"Yes, Mr President."

"About the Alien?"

"Yes, Mr President."

"I'm a busy man, George."

"Yes, Mr President."

"Why don't you start at the beginning?"

"Thank you, Mr President."

Later, after they had been brought welcome sustenance by an aide, the President eyed George over the expanse of the Resolute desk, made from the timbers of HMS Resolute and gifted by Queen Victoria in 1880. "So, George, in summary, you have had a secret friendship with two aliens for fifty years, and during that time you've been providing each other with mutual benefits."

"Yes, Mr. President."

"And on your side, most of these benefits have been for the United States of America."

"Yes, Mr President, except one Mr President."

"One, George?"

"Yes, Mr President."

"What was your benefit George?"

"In 1973 they took me to see the Horse Head Nebulae, Mr President."

"Sweet Jesus," said the President of the United States, sitting down behind his historic desk.

There was a silence between the two men that seemed to last for hours, but in reality was only minutes.

"Does anyone else know about this?"

"Only one man to my knowledge Mr President.

Colonel Charles Foxton-Smith, commander of the British Special Air Service."

"My God, Charles! I know him. He sat next to my wife at dinner once at Windsor Castle."

"Yes Mr. President."

"Well, they have gone George, your aliens. Just vanished from a cabin in Yosemite."

"They'll be back, Mr President. They always are."

"So how did it all begin?" The question died on Tupper's lips as there was a definite vibration about Polly's person. Instantly he knew what it was. "Your mobile," he said incredulously, "it works at Andromeda?"

"Of course," replied Polly with a smile, taking her “phone” from her camo pocket. "Doesn't yours?"

She studied the screen for a moment. "It's Walter," she relayed, "would we like to join them for dinner?"

"They're here? In the spaceport?"

"Sure Tupper. Let’s go and eat, I'm starving."

This was just too bizarre. Tupper, reunited with Gonzo,

had vague notions of making a break, overpowering the weirdos, and then what? Twenty years in the Regiment had taught him to be adaptable to any situation. He had been in serious shit many times, and this wasn't one of them. Jeez, he was even being fed, and then there was Polly.

Tupper suddenly realised he wasn't one hundred percent. There had been a lot of that today. Everybody around the table was looking at him waiting for a reply. Shit, he had missed the question.

"What would you like to eat?" Polly asked again.

Tupper was still remembering the wriggling stuff.

"No, really, if you could have anything, what would you have?"

"Baked beans on toast, with cheese sauce on top, the way my Mum made it," he said without thinking.

"I can't manage the last bit, but okay, good choice, and to drink?"

"A pint of 6X," said Tupper playing along with the wind up.

"I'll do my best," replied Polly, "it may taste like Butcombe Gold."

"Why?"

"My favourite."

Thirty seconds later, a waiter with translucent orange skin, a face like a fish, but impeccably dressed, brought out a tray containing a plate of beans on toast with cheese sauce, and a beaker of a cloudy amber liquid.

Tupper could smell the food and was almost as surprised by this as he had been on his arrival at the space port.

"Try it," Polly said with a smile. "The sauce is made from a proper roux with mature cheddar, just the way I like it."

Tupper was starving. Taught to take food whenever possible he wolfed it down, and then sat back in his chair, with a big smile, sipping his pint.

"I don't care how you did that, it was fantastic."

"This is the future, Tupper. I imagine what I want, and the restaurant provides. That's why I wasn't sure about the 6X. I'd rather give you something I know is right than work on a guess. Anything could happen."

"You could have done that at any time?"

"No, only when it was funny."

Tupper was so engrossed in the whole experience he had forgotten about the two weirdos and Gonzo, who were clearly enjoying this exchange. What the hell was happening to him?

`*Hey man,*' Andre's voice appeared in his head. `*Chill out, it's all cool.*'

Years of training kept his face neutral, but for the first time in decades Sergeant Alfred Smith of the SAS was feeling out of his depth.

The trouble for Polly was that a lot of guys she met didn't match up. It had been a long time since her dreadful relationship with Phillip in London. Walter and André were funny, charming, perfect gentlemen, but they were more like her two big brothers.

She looked across the table at Tupper and liked what she saw. He was ruggedly good looking with a light in his eyes, which despite the brutality she sensed they had witnessed, were sensitive, and seemed to smile at some private joke. She liked those eyes very much. She studied his face, the laugh lines around his eyes, eyes that were alive now as he listened to Walter's story about Tupper and Gonzo's boss shooting fifty rounds into a dustbin during a hostage release at a London embassy back in the early eighties.

After her experience at the Whitehall firing range, it didn't surprise her at all that Walter and Andre's friends included the commander of the world-famous Special Air Service, Major-General Charles Foxton-Smith. It must have been quite a shock to the two troopers, she thought, but if it was, their calm faces hadn't revealed it. Again, she was impressed with their easy adaptability under impossible psychological conditions.

Walter had moved onto a story about a black op in an African country where the government exerted huge influence, as it did in the constant wars that always went on somewhere on Earth. It was all down to the power of the tobacco and weapons industries, Polly knew, but Walter's story was something about a stake out in a Luanda nightclub, and an exploding parrot.

She watched the four bonding with their shared experiences of combat and ludicrous escapades, and wondered about the new dynamic, what Tupper thought about her, and how she fitted into all of this. After all it was because of Polly and Sam that swathes of London now lay in ruins, and here they were getting all pally on Andromeda.

Polly wondered about Sam too. He couldn't smell her from London to San Francisco. How was he going to find her on Andromeda?

One thing Polly was convinced of.

He surely would.

Polly smiled. The suite was wonderful. It always amazed her that the basic bed had survived into the future. Some sort of comfortable mattress, sheets, quilts, blankets, pillows. All sorts of stasis fields and three-dimensional sleep modules had developed over multiple millennia. There was one Polly had liked once where she was immersed in what she had first taken to be little warm inert beads, but had shakily realised were tiny living creatures, although they could have been robotic, how would you tell? Still the constant motion around her, whilst initially like some horror nightmare, when she meditated and let go of her conscious mind, was both stimulating and relaxing at the same time and her sleep had been deep, rejuvenating and full of beautiful dreams.

Still, for the wonderful experience she had just had you couldn't beat a large divan with silk sheets. At Andromeda's premium hotels furnishing and decor was selected like dinner, from your own experiences.

There was a quiet knock at the door, and straight away the sleeping man beside her was awake and alert.

"Did you order room service?" Tupper asked quietly.

"No. If you want food and drink, you just imagine it."

Polly looked up at the ceiling above them which transformed into a huge screen showing the corridor outside their room. Sam was standing there, his scything rows of teeth grinning broadly.

"Oh shit," said Tupper. "I don't think this is going to end well. How did he find you so fast?"

"He's very resourceful."

"And unstoppable," said Tupper, remembering their encounter in London.

"Yeah, well fortunately things are a lot stronger and better built on Andromeda. That laser cannon won't make any impression. I don't expect he will even try."

But for the second time in twenty-four hours Polly had misjudged Sam's knock at the door.

"I told you romance was in the air," said Tupper.

"Will you get dressed."

"Come on Polly, he doesn't want to fight."

"You think so, when he finds you're here?"

The sound of the explosion was simultaneous with the screen going blank. Polly staggered as the vibration rocked the room.

Tupper was knelt low behind the bed, his semi-automatic pressed into his shoulder, aiming at the door. He glanced across at Polly's naked form calmly standing, watching him, a small green gun that looked like a kid's water pistol, in her hand.

"What in God's name is that?" he asked.

"Firepower."

"Okay," he replied sceptically. Polly tossed the tiny weapon to him.

"Cover the door with this," she said as she calmly pulled on her camos and T shirt. "The door will hold, and relief is on the way."

Seconds later she was dressed and ready for action. She took her pistol back from a bemused Tupper who was tying the laces of his combat boots.

"What now?" he said but his words were lost in the explosion that blew a hole through the door. The impact of the blast smacked Tupper back into the far wall, almost making him lose consciousness from the impact and the pain. His ears rang with the clang of traumatic deafness.

In the smoking haze he saw Sam's giant form through the new hole in the wall and emptied the clip of his machine pistol, knowing the futility of it from the battle in London. In his peripheral vision he spotted movement on the floor, just in time to see an elegant hand point the tiny green pistol towards the door as Sam's terrifying visage appeared.

As a flash of exploding energy hit the alien, blowing him back and out of the opening, Tupper bounded forward, pulled Polly to her feet in a single scooping motion, and half dragging, half guiding her, ran towards the gap in the door. As if in some gymnastic display, the two of them tumbled through the smoking gap head first. Tupper had magically found time to replace the spent clip in his carbine which was firing a hail of bullets before them, whilst Polly's tiny pistol blasted out enough energy to take out a tank.

Pinned by the assault to the metallic corridor wall, the alien was looking distressed, blackened, and battered, but still very much alive and whole. The two warriors came out of their dives in a roll and raced down the corridor without looking back.

`*This way*,' Walter's voice spoke in their minds. Over the years, despite André's coaching, Polly had never completely got used to the telepathy. Tupper on the other hand took to it like a duck to water.

"Can we do that?" he gasped, as they ran along the endless corridor. Polly noticed there were no bug-eyed faces peeking out of doors, wondering what the hell was going on.

"What?" Polly replied, "telepathy?"

"Yeah, pretty useful thing in combat."

"And in the bedroom."

"Do you know that Polly?" he asked trying to keep his voice level.

"No Tupper, I don't," she panted, squeezing his free hand as she ran, "but I'd like to find out."

Their conversation was cut off by a roar behind them.

"POLLY!"

"He doesn't give up does he?"

"He does seem to be persistent. Do you think this corridor goes on forever? Where the hell are Walter and André?"

At that moment as if by magic, a door opened ahead of them, and there standing in the room were André, Walter, and Gonzo, all dressed in Hawaiian shirts, and drinking, from the smell, gin martinis from inverted pyramid shaped glasses. `*Hendricks,*' Walter popped in to her mind, knowing it was her favourite gin, and handing them both a full glass.

"What the fuck is going on?" asked Tupper.

"Cocktails," chipped in Gonzo with a smile.

"And what's with the shirts?" Tupper asked incredulously.

"Gonzo was telling us about how you guys used to dress while travelling around. We picked some up on our way to Saigon."

“Saigon,” echoed Tupper. "Have you guys any idea what is going on here?"

"Walter knows this really neat bar in 1957 run by an American buddy with a great Rock 'n Roll jukebox."

"You’re kidding me?"

"No, it was really good."

Now that the door was closed, Tupper noticed that it was very quiet, and he could no longer hear Sam's roars or the sounds of pursuit.

Sipping his drink, he settled down on a comfortable looking faux leather couch, noticing that Polly sat down beside him. He looked up at the three guys with their cocktail glasses and big smiles.

"We are safe here, aren't we?"

"Yep."

"Are we even on Andromeda now?"

"Nope."

"Then I'll have another one of these please," he said, politely holding out his glass, "and make it a double."

"It's like all warfare, in the end we need to come to a negotiated settlement."

Walter sat down and had a sip of tonic water. He looked around the small circle of faces of those sitting on deck chairs on the deserted beach. In fact, it was all beach and one palm tree. Walter had chosen a very small pacific atoll. Very small and very private. Just to be sure, he had arranged for any satellites that might be covering that remote part of the ocean to respect their solitude. As he had remarked to Tupper earlier, the military ones were easy, it was Google that had been the hardest to persuade.

"There is no warfare," put in Sam, in his perfect Oxford English, "just a misunderstanding."

"A misunderstanding," growled Tupper, "tell that to all those who have lost loved ones in London."

"Stay cool man," said André diplomatically. "Listen to the cat first, hear him out man."

"You haven't got the hots for me Sam?" said Polly.

"No Polly, I haven't got the hots for you, sorry."

"Ever the gentleman," muttered Tupper under his breath.

"Cool out man," André put in again.

"So, what were the flowers for?" asked Polly.

"To say I'm sorry."

"For blowing up half of London?"

"Alfred, you are not helping," admonished Walter firmly.

"Sorry Sam," Tupper said, his feelings for Polly mixed in with his cool unemotional detachment, and the unbelievable events of the last two days."

"What is it Sam?" asked Polly, "what is it that you're sorry for?"

"Leaving you for dead on Zega."

"But we all thought that *you* were dead."

"You may have noticed, I'm not that easy to kill."

"Couldn't you have just phoned up, or sent an email," Tupper cut in.

"Please Tupper," Polly turned to him, “it's not helping.” Turning back to Sam, she smiled for him to continue.

"When I discovered you were alive, I was beside myself. I have an honour debt to you."

Polly could feel Tupper's interjection coming, so stopped him with a glance.

"Like Tupper said. You didn't have to blow up half of London to get my attention."

"You don't understand my species Polly. Honour is like a rage in us. Anyway, don't tell me your species isn't the same. Tupper is a soldier, a killer for your leaders. Look how quickly they negotiated with me and gave you up. Walter gave me a précis of your history. Slavery, colonisation, millions exterminated."

"That doesn't excuse your behaviour Sam."

"How many times can I say it?" His orange slit eyes held her gaze over the baking sand, as he mustered all of his sincerity. "Polly, I'm really truly sorry."

Later Polly and Tupper were swimming in the warm tropical lagoon.

"Do you think Sam will come to the wedding?"

"I don't want to be a kept man Polly."

"What do you mean?"

"All those lovely homes."

"You know about those?"

"I know everything about you."

"Everything?"

"The spooks and Cheltenham are very thorough."

"Do they know what I like for breakfast?"

"No."

"Do they know where I like to have breakfast, what planets have the best sunsets?"

"I guess not."

"Do you?"

"I guess not."

"Would you like to find out?"

"Yes, I would."

"Do you know what I do with Walter and Andre?"

"Okay, I can see there are all kinds of things I don't know about Polly Granger."

"You know how to make me wriggle."

"This is true," Tupper admitted.

"And what is it that you do?"

"When?" asked Polly coyly.

"With Walter and Andre?"

"We go on adventures."

"Mind if I come along?"

"I thought you'd never ask."

THE END

PLEASE LEAVE A REVIEW

If you loved the book and have a moment to spare, I would really appreciate a short review either, at your online book store, or on Goodreads. Your help in spreading the word is gratefully appreciated and reviews make a huge difference to helping new readers find the series.

Thank you!

ANN THROPE NOVEL SERIES

ASSASSIN

She's a master of the space-time continuum. But with alien mercenaries hot on her high heels, is this assassin's life about to end in a black hole?

Sophisticated grandma Ann Thrope is exceptionally good at murder. The planet's most dangerous professional killer, she's just completed lucrative hits across the cosmos. But when word of her remarkable work spreads through the multiverse, she's saddled with a galactic-sized price on her head...

Continuing to take contracts anywhere and anywhen, Ann continues to dodge an onslaught of extraterrestrial bounty hunters. But when her grandchildren are put in the crosshairs, the stiletto-wielding senior jumps into battle to defend those she loves.

Can this classy hitwoman take down the sinister fiends on her tail before she's permanently retired?

APPRENTICE

He could have been anything when he grew up. Somehow "killer" ended up top of his list...

Young orphan Billy Brambling doesn't believe in being ordinary. Fearing life already passing him by, the eccentric nine-year-old jumps at the chance to learn how to become a deadly assassin. And with his future assured in the lethal hands of infamous hitwoman Ann Thrope, he eagerly begins his career in murder.

Studying under the sophisticated senior, a blind swordmaster, and an eight-inch fairy, Billy focuses on being the most ruthless gun-for-hire across galaxies. But when a dangerous assignment compromises his safety, the youngster must make a life-threatening choice between friend and foe.

Can the boy executioner survive a brutal alien mission, or will he come to an explosive end?

ACKNOWLEDGMENTS

Again, a big thank you to Lynn and Linda for proof reading the manuscript, and my editor Lou for all her support and amazing attention to detail.

Dan Couzens at netfrontier.co.uk Thank you for my fantastic website, **richardweale.com**

And thanks for reading my book, it's much appreciated.

Richard 2021

ABOUT THE AUTHOR

In his spare time, Richard teaches Japanese martial arts, creates images for a photography agency, and plays tenor saxophone with friends in a rock band. He lives with his partner in Gloucestershire...

Printed in Great Britain
by Amazon